THE
GREAT MOSQUITO, BULL,
AND COFFIN CAPER

THE
GREAT MOSQUITO, BULL, AND COFFIN CAPER

BY NANCY LAMB
ILLUSTRATED BY FRANK REMKIEWICZ

Lothrop, Lee & Shepard Books
New York

ACKNOWLEDGMENT

I want to thank Judit Bodnar for the
extraordinary editorial skill and insight
she contributed to this book.

First Edition 1 2 3 4 5 6 7 8 9 10

Library of Congress Cataloging in Publication Data
Lamb, Nancy. The great mosquito, bull, and coffin caper / by Nancy Lamb.
p.   cm. Summary: Hoping to create indelible memories to keep him from
forgetting his best friend Jimmy, who is moving away, ten-year-old Zander
pledges to undergo three difficult and scary ordeals with him.
ISBN 0-688-10933-0
[1. Friendship—Fiction. 2. Moving, Household—Fiction.] I. Title.
PZ7.L16725Gr 1992 [Fic]—dc20 91-31125 CIP AC

FOR MY MOTHER,
who's always taken care of me.

O N E

There are lots of things I hate in this world. I hate peas and squash and multiplication tables. I hate going to bed before I'm sleepy. I hate having a stupid older brother, too. But most of all, more than anything else in the whole world, I hate losing my best friend.

Jimmy Snyder is my best friend. Actually, we're Official Best Buddies Forever. That's higher and more powerful than best friends. Jimmy and I even look a little bit alike. We both have blue eyes and lots of freckles. But Jimmy's hair is brown. Mine is red.

Jimmy used to live two houses away from me. We could see each other from the windows of our rooms. Two years ago, when we were eight years old, we figured out a secret way to talk at night after we were supposed to be in bed. We did it with Morse code.

The night before he told me the bad news, Jimmy flashed ... ___ ... from his window. He used his special ten-year-guaranteed, lithium-battery flashlight. I have one just like it. The flashlights won't run down for eight more years. Anyway, ... ___ ... means S.O.S. And that means EMERGENCY! It was pretty late at night and Jimmy's mom must have caught him at the window. Because just as he was starting to tell me what the emergency was, the flashes stopped. I waited hours for him to start sending his message again. I guess he fell asleep.

First thing the next morning, Jimmy came over to my house. His eyes were all red and bloodshot. I could tell he'd been crying, but I pretended I didn't notice.

"What happened?" I asked.

"My dad bought a new business."

"So?"

"I'm moving," Jimmy said.

"Where?" I asked.

Jimmy swallowed hard. "Los Angeles," he croaked.

"You mean Los Angeles, *California?*" I yelled. "You're moving to CALIFORNIA?"

We lived in Austin, Oklahoma, a tiny little town in the middle of the United States. That's a long way from California.

"Just tell your parents you won't go," I said, all of a sudden feeling a big glob of tears pushing on my throat as it worked its way up to my eyes.

"I did."

"So what did they say?"

Jimmy wiped his nose with his sleeve. Then he blinked a couple of times, real hard, and sucked the tears back in his eyes like he always does when he's sad. "They said they were sorry and all that baloney, but this was a great chance for Dad to do something new because his business is get-

3

ting him down and I'd get used to my new home. But I never will. I *know* I never will."

"Your parents sure know how to ruin a person's life," I said. "They must have practiced hard to put together a ruin this big."

"Yeah," said Jimmy.

"When are you moving?" I asked, afraid to hear his answer.

"September second," Jimmy said. His voice was so low I could barely hear him.

I did some quick calculating. "That's just three weeks from now!" I yelled. The Snyders didn't even give Jimmy fair warning. Three weeks is practically nothing when it comes to changing your whole life.

"I know," said Jimmy as we walked down the block to our clubhouse.

I picked up a rock and threw it at our practice target in the empty lot.

"A long time ago," Jimmy said, "my grandpa told me about the best friend he had when he was our age. His friend moved away and they never talked to each other again."

4

"That won't ever happen to us," I said, trying to imagine what my life would be like without Jimmy. Who would I tell my secrets to? I thought. Who would camp out with me on my birthday or choose me first when we divided up sides for baseball teams? "We'll never let it happen."

"I sure hope not," said Jimmy. He didn't sound very confident.

That night, the first thing my big brother, Marvin, said to me was, "Hi, Non. I heard Jimmy's moving."

"Yeah," I said glumly.

"He'll forget you in a week," Marvin said.

I don't know which made me angrier: being called Non or being teased about Jimmy forgetting me.

Maybe I should explain. My name isn't Non. It's Zander. That's short for Alexander. Alexander Caulfield. But when Marvin wants to bug me without going to very much trouble, he calls me his own special nickname. Just to show you how nasty my sleazy brother is, as soon as I get used to one nickname, he gives me a new one. I've already been Thon and Tron and McTron and McNon and Non.

I'm just about used to Non now. So I guess one of these days real soon I'll be getting a new name. You'd think that after all this time and all those names it wouldn't bug me anymore. But it does.

As you can probably tell, Marvin is a fungus growing on my life. He's nasty and ugly and I can't get rid of him. Just because he's twelve years old, his allowance is seventy-five cents bigger than mine. He gets to go to bed one whole hour later than me, too. And as if that's not enough, he talks like a genius and keeps reminding me in this really snotty way that he's got this incredible I.Q. But this is the clincher: No matter what he does or what I do, Marvin always fixes things so I get the blame.

TWO

"Marvin says we'll forget each other a week after you move," I told Jimmy the next morning in the clubhouse.

"No way," said Jimmy.

"Do you think it's possible?" I asked. "Is it that easy to forget someone when they live far away?"

Jimmy thought about it. "Not if you've done something together that's hard to forget," he said. "And we've done lots of important things together."

That's what gave me the idea. "What if we did something really *weird* together, something absolutely *impossible* to forget," I said. "If it was scary enough, if it was awful enough, we'd be sure to remember it as long as we live."

"And no matter how far away we are or how old we are, we'd remember the same weird thing. And then we'd remember each other. Right?"

"Right!" I said.

"That's a great idea!" said Jimmy. "It's got to be a secret, though. Nobody else can have our memory besides us."

"It will be like an invisible string. Till the day we die, we'll be tied together," I said. "We'll be the only two people in the whole world who know about this special thing that's stretched between us forever!"

We both agreed it was a great idea. But after we talked awhile, we decided one special thing wasn't good enough. Two things would be better. But three things would be best of all. Because even if we forgot one or two, we would never forget three awesome things.

Then I thought of something important.

9

"If we decide on three things we have to do, each one should be harder than the last. Number three should be practically impossible."

"Yeah," said Jimmy. "The first one ought to be pretty easy, though. We gotta work up to the big one."

"Right," I agreed.

"We can call it The Great Best Buddy Forever Challenge," Jimmy said.

It took us a week to figure out what the three challenges would be. The first one was the Killer Mosquito Test.

THREE

"Me and Jimmy are going out to play!" I yelled to Mom the day of the Killer Mosquito Test. Then I ran out the back door.

"Who?" she called out to me. I was pretty sure she heard me.

"Me and Jimmy!" I said. By then, Mom had come to the back door and was standing about one inch away from me.

"Who?" she said again, louder this time.

"Me and *Jimmy!*" I shouted. Then I got it.

I figured I'd never get away from the house if I didn't say it right. So I said it nice and slow. Very slow. "Jimmy and *I* are going out to play." I looked at her real hard while I talked. Mothers can be so stupid sometimes.

"That's better," Mom said. She smiled at me, all nice, like she didn't know how mad she made me. "Have fun. I love you."

I didn't say I loved her back.

Anyway, *me* and Jimmy met at the corner. Then we walked down to Cow Creek where we planned to do the first challenge.

We took the short cut through Danny Lain's field. Everywhere we stepped, hundreds of grasshoppers jumped out of the high, yellow grass. The air was so hot and dry it almost cracked.

When we got to Cow Creek, we had to walk a long way to find a place to cross the stream.

The water was shallow. We could have waded across, but the creek was full of thick, gooey mud and quicksand. Sometimes it's hard to tell which is which. I got caught in the quicksand once. That stuff really sucks you down fast. It's a good thing my father was there to pull me out. Anyway, the quicksand is why me and Jimmy didn't just walk across the creek, even though we were in a hurry to get to the other side for the Killer Mosquito Test.

We climbed seven rocks and jumped over eleven puddles before we found a tree that had fallen across the middle of the creek. It made a perfect bridge.

After we crawled to the other side of the creek, it didn't take long to find the pool where the mosquitos hang out. It was really just a big, shallow puddle. The water was nasty and smelly, and the mosquitos loved it. When we got close to the puddle, we saw a whole swarm of insects flying above the water.

When I was in fourth grade, I wrote a five-and-a-half-page report about mosquitos. The humming noise they make is the sound of their wings beating about a thousand times a second! I can't even count to ten in one second.

If you hear the humming stop all of a sudden, it means some hungry critter has landed on you and is drinking your blood for breakfast. Yuck!

To pass the Killer Mosquito Test, Jimmy and I decided we had to let a mosquito drink our blood. And we weren't allowed to slap it, or anything like that. We just had to stand there and watch.

To be honest, Jimmy and I thought that would be pretty easy to do. That's why we chose it for the first Challenge. We figured it had to be easier than the bull or the coffins.

"You want to go first?" I asked, hoping Jimmy would want the honor.

"Naw," he said. "You go ahead."

Just my luck to have a generous friend, I thought, as a tiny feather of fear tickled my stomach.

I swallowed hard and walked over to the puddle. Then I got real close and stuck my arm right into the mess of mosquitos. I'm not exaggerating when I tell you that those suckers pounced on me like robins on a June bug. I guess they were hungry.

Now, like I said, I studied about mosquitos. First of all, both male and female mosquitos sip plant juices for food. Unfortunately, female mosquitos aren't satisfied with that. They also like blood. That's why they bite. Actually, it's more like giving a shot than biting. Mosquitos have this thing called a proboscis. It's sort of like a long nose. On the end of this proboscis there are six tiny needles called stylets. Well, the lady mosquito just pokes those stylets right through your skin and rams them into the nearest blood vessel. To keep your blood from clotting up so it doesn't get too thick to drink, she has a special chemical in her saliva. The chemical drips inside your skin and keeps your blood running nice and thin and tasty. Saliva is just a fancy word for spit. And it's the mosquito's spit that makes you itch.

Now, when I stuck my hand near the swarm of Cow Creek mosquitos, about fifty of them landed on my arm.

"Yikes!" I screamed when I saw them settling in for a regular Thanksgiving feast. "I'll be eaten alive!"

I haven't moved so fast since the day Marvin put a garter snake in my lunch box. With a couple of slaps of my other hand, I massacred as many mosquitos as I could. Then I jumped up and down and swung my arms and kicked my feet, figuring it would be harder for them to attack a moving target.

When I finally calmed down, Jimmy said, "You were probably too close to the swarm. You made it too easy for them, that's all. If we stand over by the trees, maybe they'll come one at a time."

"Yeah," I said.

"You gotta do it again," Jimmy said.

"I did it already!" I said.

"But you didn't do it right."

"There were too many of them!" I protested.

"But you didn't follow the rules."

Even though Jimmy was right, I didn't think it was fair to ask me to do it over again. "I *sorta* followed the rules," I said.

"Sorta's not the same," Jimmy said in his official, rule-following voice.

I thought about it for a minute. "I guess you're right," I said. "I'll do it over. But I gotta rest a minute. You go ahead and take your turn."

"Sure." He was real cool. I couldn't tell if he was pretending or if he really wasn't scared.

I kept moving around, but Jimmy stood still. In no time, a mosquito landed on his leg.

"Look!" he said.

I bent over and watched. The mosquito got comfortable and then dug right in.

"Don't you hate it?" I asked.

"Yeah," Jimmy said. "But it's not as bad as I thought. I don't feel a thing."

"Just wait," I said, thinking of all that itchy spit.

After the mosquito finished with lunch, she flew off.

"I did it!" Jimmy said with a great big smile.

"Yeah."

"Now it's your turn."

"Are you sure the other one doesn't

count?" I asked. "There were at least a hundred of them on me. I probably got lots of bites."

"Naw. They never had time to bite. You wiped them out before they could do any damage."

"I hope so," I said.

"You scared?"

"Not really," I said. "I just don't like it, that's all."

"I was a little bit scared," Jimmy admitted.

"I know what you mean," I said, glad Jimmy was the kind of friend who could tell me something like that. I don't like being scared all alone.

"So are you going to do it now?" Jimmy asked.

"Sure."

I wanted to get it over with, quick, so I moved closer to the puddle. Then I stood still and listened real carefully. Sure enough, I heard that high mosquito hum. Then there was silence. I scanned my body, but I didn't see anything.

"She's on me somewhere," I said. "I know she is."

"I dunno. I don't see her," said Jimmy.

We were silent a minute, just looking and listening.

"There she is!" Jimmy pointed to the top of my arm.

I wasn't wearing a shirt because it was too hot. I looked high up on my left arm and my eyeballs practically landed on top of this gigantic mosquito. I was so close I could see everything. I watched her get comfortable. She moved her proboscis around like she was searching for the tenderest spot with the tastiest blood. Then she dug right in, just poked me with that stupid needle nose of hers and settled down for dinner. I got sort of dizzy thinking about all those little stylets sticking inside me. And when I remembered that the proboscis was like a long nose, I wondered if she was getting snot all over me, too.

Eccckh! Just the thought of that made me want to puke. And on top of the snot, this bug, this insect, was spitting in me! I wanted to slap her hard and send her on to

Mosquito Heaven. But I held onto my control. If I hadn't, Jimmy and I couldn't be Official Best Buddies Forever.

It seemed like the mosquito was eating a ten-course meal. I could actually see that bug's stomach filling with my blood. After about fifteen minutes she pulled her nose out and started to fly away. She was so heavy she moved like an overloaded cargo plane that can't get off the runway. She flapped and flapped her wings. Finally she took off.

"She's finished!" I said.

"Congratulations!"

I clapped my hands together. By accident the mosquito got in the way. But I didn't feel too bad. After all, it was *my* blood that squished in a red splotch all over my palms.

That night when Jimmy and I were sending messages with our flashlights, he said, "I have ten bites."

I flashed back my message:

·· ···· ·— ···— · ··· ·· —··— — · · —·

I guess we forgot to pay attention to the

rest of our bodies when we were watching the mosquitos bite us. We probably lost a pint of blood. But worse than that, I looked like I'd been attacked by a measles monster. And I itched like crazy!

But when I think of it now, that itching was a piece of cake compared to our next test.

FOUR

"Hey, Ness!" Marvin called to me.

I pretended I didn't hear him.

"Hey, Nessie!" Marvin said.

That's it, I thought. My brother has stooped to a new low. He's actually named me after a slimy, scaly sea monster.

Marvin tapped me on the shoulder. "I'm talking to you," he said.

"My name's Zander," I told him.

"Perhaps that's true for the general public," Marvin said in his super snotty voice. "But I'm not one of the masses, and I intend to call you Ness."

"So what?" I said, as angry tears stung my eyes. I knew if I didn't get out of the kitchen quick, I'd start crying. So I walked out the back door as casually as I could, then ran down the block to the clubhouse.

So Ness is my new name, I thought. Marvin probably changed it from Non because I put Saran Wrap across the toilet seat because he told Mom I said the *S* word in front of Mrs. Duncan. He did that because I borrowed his new bike without asking. I can't remember what he did to me before that. Or what I did to him before that.

But the way things look, we'll probably go on taking turns getting back at each other forever. And fifty years from now when we've grown into hopeless wrinklies, we'll probably still be thinking up new ways to get even.

Anyway, the Saran Wrap revenge made a pretty big mess. I was a little bit surprised that Marvin cleaned it up without telling Mom. But I just figured he was too embarrassed to admit he'd done something so stupid. How could I know that he was only saving his ammunition for the big gun?

"I bet you can't peel and eat three hard-boiled eggs in two minutes," he said to me the next afternoon.

"How much do you want to bet?" I asked.

He looked at me like he was sizing up my peeling and eating skills. Then he said, "Here's the deal. You have to take three eggs, crack them on your head like you always do, then peel and eat them in two minutes. If you can do that, I'll give you a dollar."

I sure needed that dollar. Because Jimmy and I had a special plan, and we needed some money to make it happen. I tried to calculate how long it would take me to crack and peel and eat an egg. I figured I could do it in about forty-five seconds. Three times forty-five seconds is two minutes and fifteen seconds. But then I figured I could stuff the whole egg in my mouth and be eating that one while I was cracking and peeling the next one. I could run into a bit of trouble if I got one of those eggs that just doesn't want to be peeled. Even then, it would be close, but I thought I could do it.

"You'll give me a dollar if I can peel and eat three eggs in two minutes," I said. "But what happens if I lose?"

"You pay me a dollar."

I hesitated. "No way," I said. "I'm not the one who made up the bet. It's not worth it." Then I turned and walked away, a bargaining technique I learned from Marvin himself.

"All right," Marvin said. "It's a one-sided bet, then. I'll give you a dollar if you win. And you don't have to pay me anything if you lose."

Yes! I thought, very proud of myself for doing such a good job of negotiating.

Marvin nodded. "Let's go."

As we started down the stairs, Marvin said, "I'll go get the dollar, just to make everything legitimate."

"Good thinking," I said.

I was waiting in the kitchen when Marvin

walked in and waved the dollar in my face. Then he set it on the counter.

"Now, here's what we'll do," Marvin said. He reached into the refrigerator and picked up three eggs from the bowl of hard-boiled eggs Mom keeps for us. "Here are the eggs. I'll put them right here on the counter." Marvin gently laid them in a row. "We'll stand right by the sink so you can drop the shells in there. And we can both watch the clock since it's right in front of us."

"Good," I said.

"Are you ready?"

I wiggled my feet to place them just right. Then I poised my hand over the first egg and watched the clock. "Go!" Marvin said as the second hand swept past twelve.

I grabbed the first hard-boiled egg, smashed it against my forehead just about where my hair begins, and rolled it backwards and forwards. I have lots of experience cracking eggs this way. Even though Mom says it's gross, it's fun to hear the shells popping against my head.

I cracked the first egg in less than ten

seconds. Then I started peeling. I was in luck: This was one of those eggs where the whole shell just sort of slips right off. Quick as a flash, I shoved the egg into my mouth and grabbed the next egg. I was ahead of schedule. My heart pounded like a jackhammer as I tried to mash the egg against the roof of my mouth so I could chew it and crack the next egg on top of my head at the same time.

I still had a mouthful of mush when I finished peeling the second egg. I should have worked a glass of water into the contest rules. I needed to wash the egg down. But I knew Marvin would scream "Foul!" if I tried to sip something. So I swallowed the last of the first egg and then tried to work up a little spit before I popped the second egg in my mouth.

A whole minute had passed. I had to hurry. So I popped the second egg into my mouth and grabbed the third egg off the counter. I had a mouthful of mush when I cracked the third egg on my forehead and rolled it backwards.

"AARRGGH!" I screamed, spewing mushed, half-eaten egg all over the counter and wall as slimy, snotty, disgusting raw egg began to drip down my forehead and mix in my hair. "AAAGRGGGAGHHH!"

I turned to Marvin. His face was redder than an autumn apple. I could tell he was trying not to laugh. He actually looked like he was going to explode.

"What happened?" he asked, all wide-eyed and innocent.

Then it hit me like a hurricane: not just a smell. A terrible, nasty, slimy, vomity stench. I had never smelled a rotten egg before. But there was not one smidgin of doubt in my mind that what I had just smashed on my forehead and squashed into my hair was a rotten egg. Because it was the most disgusting, revolting, repulsive smell that had ever crawled into my nose.

"You creep!" I screamed at Marvin. "You nasty, rotten, good-for-nothing, sneaky, lying creep!" Tears streamed

down my face and mixed with rotten-egg
goo on my cheeks.

"Time's up," Marvin said, eying the
clock as he grabbed his dollar off the
counter. "You lose the bet."

I scooped some glops of egg off my face
and lunged toward Marvin, trying to wipe
the stinky slime on his arm. But he knew
what was coming, because he laughed a
nasty, teasing laugh before he ran out the
door into the backyard.

Just then Mom walked into the kitchen.

"What's going on?" she asked. Then

she put on her brakes and her face screwed up into a tangle of disgusted wrinkles. "What's that awful smell?" she asked.

I swallowed. "Rotten egg. Marvin made me mash it on my head."

Mom raised her eyebrows. "Marvin *made* you mash a rotten egg on your head?"

"Well, not exactly. We had this bet, see? And he laid out the eggs. And he sneaked this rotten egg in with the others. And I cracked it on my head like I always do."

Mom nodded and sighed.

"Here," she said, scooting the step stool over to the sink. "Lean over and let me wash the egg out of your hair."

I stepped up on the stool and Mom took the spray attachment and squirted water all over my head.

"I'll have to use detergent, since we don't have any shampoo here," she said. "You'll probably need that, anyway, in order to get rid of the stench."

Mom soaped and rinsed my hair three times. But when she finished, I could still smell the egg.

"That's probably because some of the

31

egg is on the floor and counter," she said. "I'll help you clean it up."

Just as we finished wiping the counters, Marvin walked real casually in the kitchen door.

"You creep!" I yelled at him. "You stupid lame-brain creep!"

Marvin smiled his nastiest smile. "*I'm* a lame-brain?" he asked.

"Just exactly what did you have to do with this?" Mom asked Marvin.

"All I did was make a bet that Zander couldn't peel and eat three hard-boiled eggs in two minutes," Marvin said, as if he were an innocent, newborn baby.

"And Zander just happened to crack a rotten egg on his head?" Mom said.

"Right," Marvin agreed.

"And you had nothing to do with it," Mom said.

"Right," Marvin said again.

"There just happened to be an unboiled, rotten egg in the bowl where I keep the hard-boiled eggs for you and Zander to eat."

32

"Right," said Marvin.

"Wrong," said Mom.

I wanted to jump up and down and cheer.

Marvin looked at the floor. He didn't say a word.

"You put that egg there, Marvin. I know you did. You've probably been saving it for months in the back of your closet, just waiting for the right opportunity to sucker your little brother into this bet."

I winced when Mom said I'd been "suckered." She was right, of course. But I didn't exactly like to hear it in a public announcement.

"Go to your room, Marvin," Mom said in her quiet, don't-mess-with-me voice. "Right this instant. I want you to stay there for the rest of the day."

"But I'm going to the movies this afternoon with Noah and Ben," Marvin protested.

"Your plans have changed. Call them. Tell them you can't go. Because you're grounded until tomorrow morning."

Marvin knew he was cornered. So he shot me a nasty look and then stomped off in a huff to his room.

This is great, I thought. Mom is mad, really mad. And for once her mad isn't pointed at me.

There was only one problem. I still stank.

After I changed clothes, I went to meet Jimmy at our clubhouse so we could make plans for step two of the Great Best Buddy Forever Challenge.

Our clubhouse was in an empty lot at the end of our block. Jimmy and I dug it all by ourselves.

When I got five feet away from the entrance, I stomped my foot three times, looked around to make certain I was alone, and then said our secret password: "Hi Lo Ini Mini Ki Ki, Um Chi Chi E Wa Wa."

Jimmy and I made up the words ourselves. Lots of different times, Marvin had tried to find out what the password was. That's because Jimmy and I wouldn't raise the clubhouse door for anyone who didn't know the secret words. And we sure weren't stupid enough to say them out loud when Marvin was around.

When we weren't in the clubhouse, Jimmy and I kept the trapdoor padlocked. We chained the door to a thick wooden stake with a hole in it. We put the stake in the ground with cement we mixed ourselves. That, plus the pile of dirt and rocks on the roof, made the place pretty secure. Even though he pretended like he didn't care, Marvin used to get really annoyed that he couldn't see inside.

Anyway, when Jimmy heard the password, he opened the clubhouse door.

As soon as I jumped down inside, Jimmy looked at me like I had just grown an extra ear. "What's that smell?" he asked, sniffing the air.

"Egg," I said. "Rotten egg."

"Rotten egg? Why on earth do you smell like a rotten egg?" Jimmy asked, like I had just snapped my twig.

I sighed, a little embarrassed, even in

front of my best friend. "Marvin made this bet with me about cracking and peeling and eating three eggs in two minutes," I said, feeling really stupid.

"And you cracked the eggs on your head the way you always do," Jimmy said, shaking his head.

"Right."

"And he tricked you into smashing a rotten egg on the top of your head," Jimmy said.

"Right."

Jimmy patted me on the shoulder. It was nice of him not to tell me how stupid I was to fall for another one of Marvin's tricks.

"Well, a little stink from a rotten egg can't keep us from making plans for the next challenge," Jimmy said as he crawled over to the trap door and opened it. The fresh air helped dilute the stink.

"Right," I said.

"Okay. I'll bring the red cloth and you bring the canteen of water," Jimmy said. "It's a long walk to Charlie Baker's farm."

"Yeah," I answered. "I'll bring the big canteen."

"You want to do it day after tomorrow?" Jimmy asked.

"Sure," I said. And I felt a terrible dread dig deep into the pit of my stomach.

FIVE

I was the first one in the clubhouse the next morning. I heard three stomps on the ground. Then Jimmy said the secret password real fast: "Hi Lo Ini Mini Ki Ki, Um Chi Chi E Wa Wa."

I scrambled to the trapdoor and pushed it up.

"Quick!" Jimmy said. "Marvin's following me!"

He jumped down into the clubhouse and slammed the trapdoor. If we kept our voices low, we knew Marvin couldn't hear us once the door was in place. We had tested it.

"I brought lights," Jimmy said, handing me some candles.

"Good thinking," I replied.

We stuck the three green candles, probably left over from Christmas, in the dirt and lit them. The light from the flames flickered back and forth, making our cave seem haunted and mysterious. It reminded me of horror movies on TV.

"Did you get the red cloth?" I asked.

"Naw. I looked through every shelf in my mom's sewing room. But she's already packed a lot of stuff, and I couldn't find a piece of red cloth anywhere. Not even a scrap. So I brought these," he said, sort of embarrassed, as he reached under his shirt and pulled out a pair of red pajamas decorated with barnyard animals. Chickens and ducks and horses and cows roamed all over Jimmy's fire-engine-red pajamas.

"Well, they *are* red," I said, shaking my head. I didn't tell him how stupid-looking the pajamas were. Because stupid's the only kind Jimmy's ever had. I don't know why, but his mom gets a little nuts when it comes to choosing material for things like that.

"Do you think those will work?" I asked doubtfully.

"Beats me," said Jimmy. "I've never done anything like this before. But red's supposed to be the right color, the one that makes them really mad."

"I'm a little nervous," I said.

"Me, too," he said. "But we'd better get used to that. Because if we can't pull this one off, we're sure as heck not going to be brave enough to do the third Challenge."

"Yeah. I guess you're right," I said. "I'm having bad dreams about that already. Maybe we should just skip the last one."

"*Not do the third Challenge?*" Jimmy said, like he couldn't believe his ears. Jimmy always follows the rules. "If we change the third Challenge to something easier, we might not remember it when we're grown-ups. And if we forget our tests, we might forget each other. Then we won't be Official Best Buddies Forever. Besides," he added, "we made a pact and we should stick to it."

I sighed, resigning myself to the fact that I would probably be dead by the end of the month. "All right," I said, changing the subject because I was starting to get the creeps. "I've got a dollar seventy-five now for the lockbox," I told Jimmy. "I cleaned the Kitty Litter tray four times this week for a dollar. Phew! That's a nasty job!"

"Well, I have two sixty-six. I found a penny on the sidewalk."

"Let me see," I said, scratching $2.66 and $1.75 in the dirt so I could add them up. "That's four dollars and forty-one cents. The lockbox costs five ninety-five. We're almost there," I said, doing subtraction in the dirt. "We just need another dollar and fifty-four cents."

"That shouldn't be too hard to earn."

"What about tax?"

"Throw in another quarter. That makes it a dollar seventy-nine," I said. "Make it another twenty-six cents. Then it's an even dollar-eighty. So if we each earn another ninety cents, that'll do it."

Jimmy nodded. "I can get fifty cents for sweeping the sidewalk and the driveway. The trouble is, I did it yesterday and everything's still clean."

"Maybe we could throw some dirt on it," I suggested.

"Come on, Zander. That's cheating!"

"Yeah," I said. I'm not *perfect,* after all.

"We gotta come up with the money some way," Jimmy said.

"Too bad we don't have something to sell."

That's when Jimmy got the idea. "I

know! Why don't we sell Marvin that old *Green Lantern* comic my cousin gave me?"

"Sell him your *comic?*" I said. I hated to think of a friend of mine selling something special just so we could have a lockbox.

"Think about it this way," said Jimmy. "I didn't even know it was valuable till Marvin started collecting comics. Besides," he added, "we've both practically memorized it."

"Yeah," I said.

"You think Marvin would actually buy it?" Jimmy asked. "He's awfully stingy."

"I think he might," I said. "I know he wants that comic. Because a couple of days ago he told me he was saving for a mint-condition *Green Lantern* that the guy at Ray's Used Books is selling for ten dollars."

"Wow," Jimmy said. "That's a lot of money for a comic."

"It is," I said. "But that's mint condition. Perfect. No creases or tears or anything."

"Well, there's no doubt about it: My

43

Green Lantern is definitely not in mint condition," Jimmy said. "So we should probably sell it to Marvin cheap."

"Oh, I don't know," I said. "Don't forget the egg."

"Yeah," said Jimmy, nodding. "The egg."

Later that morning, Jimmy and I read his *Green Lantern* for the last time. Then we put it under a couple of heavy boxes for an hour, figuring that might press a few wrinkles out.

"I don't think it worked," I said to Jimmy as we inspected the comic after its mashing.

"Me neither," I said.

"All we really need is a dollar eighty," said Jimmy. "How much do you think we ought to ask for it?"

"Oh, I don't know," I said. "But I do know this: Whatever we ask, we should add some money onto the price. Then Marvin can tell us he won't pay that much, and when we give it to him for less, he'll think he got a bargain."

"Good thinking!" said Jimmy.

"Guess where I got the idea," I said. "He's done it to me a million times."

Jimmy and I found Marvin standing in front of the open refrigerator staring at the food. He had the same hypnotized look on his face that he gets when he watches "Twilight Zone" reruns.

"Hey, Marvin," Jimmy said. "You want to buy my *Green Lantern?*"

That got Marvin's attention real fast. "Where is it?" he said, coming out of his trance as he closed the refrigerator door.

"Here," said Jimmy, handing him the comic.

Marvin conducted a silent examination of every nook and cranny in the book. As he turned the pages, he kept shaking his head like he couldn't believe what he was seeing. After he finished his inspection, he looked at Jimmy and asked, "How much do you want for this mutilated comic?"

"Four fifty," Jimmy answered.

"No way!" said Marvin. "This is in terrible condition. Look at all the creases! And there's even a dog-eared corner! I'm surprised it's not missing some pages."

"But it's not," I said.

"I'll give you a dollar fifty," said Marvin.

I resisted the temptation to glance at Jimmy. We didn't expect Marvin to start so high. But Jimmy and I had rehearsed the bargaining routine several times and he knew what to do. We had already decided that we'd settle for two dollars, so we didn't have very far to go.

"I said four fifty and I meant it," Jimmy said firmly, like he wouldn't take a penny less.

"How about two dollars?" said Marvin.

I thought Jimmy would accept Marvin's offer right then and there. But instead he said, "How about four dollars?"

"Two fifty?" said Marvin.

Take it! I thought. Don't be stupid! That's a fifty-cent profit!

"Three fifty," said Jimmy.

"Two sixty," Marvin said.

I held my breath, hoping Jimmy wouldn't turn down this offer. I tried to send him a message by E.S.P.

"Absolutely not," said Jimmy.

"Two seventy-five," Marvin said.

I felt like I was watching a tennis match.

"Nope," said Jimmy like he did this all the time. "I won't take a penny less than three dollars."

He's blown it! I thought. Now he's made Marvin mad and we'll never sell the comic.

"All right," said Marvin. "Three dollars."

Jimmy and Marvin shook hands. Then I looked at Jimmy and said, "You're a genius."

"Wrong," said Marvin. "Lest you forget, *I'm* the genius."

S I X

Ready for the second Challenge, I met Jimmy in the clubhouse at eight the next morning. We grabbed the red barnyard pajamas and the canteen, then started out for Charlie Baker's farm. We didn't waste any time because it was a long walk and we wanted to get there before the sun got too hot. Oklahoma summers can be real body boilers. Just in case we had to escape real fast, we didn't want to do it by melting.

The sky was a clear, pale blue, exactly the color of the best shooter marble I ever had. Fields of grass stretched all the way to the horizon, straw colored and parched, decorated by clumps of stubborn green trees that somehow managed to grow along the muddy creek beds.

Charlie Baker's farm was over three miles out of town. Mr. Baker raised cattle. Not just any old cattle. Prize cattle, ones he entered in state fair contests and things like that. Most cattle just look like regular cows to me. But Charlie Baker had this one bull that was really awesome. He was a Brahman bull, the kind that has long, curved, pointed horns on its head and a big hump on its back. No matter what he ever did, that bull always looked like he was in a mean, rotten mood.

Jimmy and I were still probably a quarter of a mile away from the Baker farm when I looked across the field and saw the bull standing in the shade of a cottonwood tree.

"There he is," I said.

"I hope he's in a good mood today," Jimmy whispered, as if he didn't want to make any noise that might annoy the monster.

"Me, too," I said, suddenly wondering if

49

I had totally lost my mind. After all, this wasn't some old milk cow named Bessie. This was a humongous Brahman bull, the kind that people pay thousands of dollars to mate with their cow so they can make more humongous, prize-winning Brahman bulls. And on top of that, people around here have been saying for years that the Bakers' bull was meaner than a rattlesnake with a bellyache.

"I dunno," I said as I stared across the pasture. "That sucker looks mighty big to me."

"You're right," Jimmy agreed. "I didn't remember that it was so huge."

"Me neither."

"That just makes the Challenge more exciting," Jimmy said, like a total dweeb.

"Sure," I said, leaning over to scrunch under the barbed-wire fence that Jimmy held up for me. Then, when I got to the other side, I held the wire up for him.

As we walked toward the bull, I began to feel like I was walking my last mile.

"You want the tops or the bottoms?"

Jimmy asked as we walked across the pasture.

"Huh?"

"You want the tops or bottoms?" he repeated.

"Of what?"

"The pajamas, of course," Jimmy said, sort of annoyed.

"I'll take the tops," I said, figuring they didn't look quite as silly as the bottoms. After all, when you're walking to your doom, you don't want to give up *all* your dignity.

We approached the bull from the side. The closer we got, the scarier he looked. And the bigger he got. I glanced around, measuring in my mind the distance to the fence and checking to see if there were any trees between the fence and me, just in case I had to climb one fast. There wasn't even one.

"So what do we do now?" I whispered.

Jimmy swallowed. His lips looked like they were sticking together. "Gimme the canteen," he croaked.

51

I took the canteen off my belt and handed it to him. Jimmy took a big swig, then wiped his mouth with his forearm before giving me back the bottle. I took a gulp. The water felt good trickling down my dust-dried throat.

Jimmy took a deep breath.

"What we do now is move a little closer and then start the two-man bullfight," he said.

SEVEN

That bull's bigger than a brontosaurus, I thought. And fifty times bigger than Jimmy and me. The monster was only about twenty feet away. My knees started to shake, and for a minute I thought I'd puke.

"When I say 'Go,' lift your cape and wave it," Jimmy whispered.

My cape? I thought as I looked at the pajamas. That bullfight Jimmy saw on TV has really affected him. The kid's not playing with a full deck. On the other hand, I added to myself, I guess I'm not, either. Anybody who stands in front of a two-thousand-pound Brahman bull and waves a pair of red pajama tops has got to be missing a few neurons.

"One . . . two . . . three . . . ," Jimmy whispered, "Go!"

I stood in front of the bull, paralyzed with fear. Jimmy looked at me. "Aren't you gonna do it?" he asked.

"I . . . I . . . ," I croaked.

"You can do it!" Jimmy said. I don't know how he found his voice. "Come on—lift up your cape!"

Like a robot following programmed directions, I raised my hands. The pajamas hung limp in front of me.

Jimmy stood tall, his back arched and his feet together, holding his cape out to his side like a genuine Spanish matador. *"Olé!"* he cried, waving the silly barnyard pajama bottoms. The legs of the pants flapped wildly with every move of his waving arms. *"Olé!"*

The bull switched his tail from side to side as he gazed out over the pasture.

"Maybe he's blind," I said. "I don't think he even sees us."

"You could be right," said Jimmy. "But

don't give up yet." He straightened his shoulders, then yelled, "Hey! *Olé!*"

"*Olé!*" I echoed softly.

The bull sighed, totally uninterested in our antics.

"Maybe he's deaf, too," said Jimmy. "I don't think he even hears us."

"He's probably fifty years old and ready for the grave," I said.

"*Olé!*" Jimmy cried.

"Yeah! *Olé!*" I echoed, my voice a little stronger now that I saw the bull wasn't going to charge me. I waved the red pajamas in front of the utterly bored beast.

"Let's do it together," Jimmy said. "Ready?"

I nodded.

"One . . . two . . . three . . ."

"*OLÉ!*" we screamed, frantically waving our capes. "*OLÉ! OLÉ! OLÉ!*"

The bull turned away from us like we were two annoying flies nipping at his hump.

"No doubt about it. He's deaf and blind and senile," I said. "This isn't working at all."

"No kidding," Jimmy said, totally disgusted. "This bull wouldn't know a bullfight from a baseball game."

"I guess bulls aren't very smart," I said.

"Well, at least we tried."

"In spite of the fact that we didn't actually have a bullfight, we probably won't forget it, anyway," I said, feeling very relieved. "After all, how many times in our life are we going to stand in front of a blind and deaf Brahman bull and wave a pair of red barnyard pajamas?"

"I guess you're right," Jimmy said. "Even though we flopped, we'll remember it." He kicked the dirt with the toe of his sneaker, raising a small cloud of red dust. "Come on," he said. "Let's get out of here."

I looked at the bull one more time. "You're a wimp," I said, then turned toward home.

"Probably this Challenge turned out easy," Jimmy said, "because our next one is going to be so hard."

"Probably." I didn't want to think about the coffins.

Hot and dejected, Jimmy and I walked across the crackling dry pasture, dragging our pitiful red barnyard pajama halves behind us.

"What a bummer," I said. "After all that, after being so scared, after thinking I was gonna puke, what a bummer."

"Right."

We walked along in silence, totally depressed. I guess it's lucky we were so quiet. Because if we had been talking, we might not have heard the noise.

"What's that?" I asked. A rhythmic, pounding sound vibrated the hot, dry air.

"Beats me," Jimmy said. He looked really down in the dumps.

I glanced around.

"Oh, no," I moaned. "Oh, no!"

What I saw horrified me. Because that stupid, ancient, blind, deaf, wimpy Brahman bull was coming down on us like a runaway train.

"Run!" I screamed. *"Run for the fence!"*

EIGHT

Jimmy looked around and saw the bull closing in on us.

"Aaaaggghh!" he screamed, and then took off like he had a jet engine strapped to his back.

Driven by panic and a powerful desire to see another sunset, we ran faster than racehorses on Derby Day.

Trouble was, the bull ran faster. I didn't take the time to look around. But I could tell he was getting closer because the ground started to shake. And it didn't take much brain power to figure out that the

shaking wasn't caused by Jimmy and me. Finally I couldn't stand it any longer. I glanced around. The stampeding bull was practically on top of us, his mean, red eyes focused right on me.

The fence was at least a block away. At the rate that bull was going, we weren't gonna make it.

"Split!" I screamed over the thunderous noise, hoping that dividing the target in two would confuse the animal. *"Split up!"*

Dropping the pajama tops, I took off to the left. Screaming with terror, Jimmy cut to the right.

My side felt like it was going to split. And my throat turned drier than a mummy's mouth. I was fresh out of spit, but that didn't stop me. Once I was out of the bull's path, I sprinted so fast I scorched the green right off the grass, heading straight for the fence like my life depended on it. As a matter of fact, it did.

I guess the bull liked me. Because when he had to choose between Jimmy and me, he chose me. He probably thought I'd be more fun to toss around on his horns or something. Anyway, he veered to the left and followed me, trying to cut me off before I reached the fence. The noise from his crashing hooves was so loud it sounded like I was about to be run over by a monster truck.

"Aiieeee!" I screamed as I dived for the fence. I wiggled under the barbed wire and rolled into the ditch on the other side. I looked up just in time to see Jimmy slide under the fence. He turned around to pull the red pajama bottoms through, but they caught on the barbs and tore into shreds.

Catching sight of the fence, the monster bull slammed on his brakes and started to skid. A smoky cloud of dust swirled up around him like he was laying fifty feet of tread marks on a long, flat highway. I could almost smell burning rubber. He stood on the other side of the barbed wire huffing and puffing, his mean red headlight eyes glaring at me like he was just dying to poke his horns right through my belly button.

I couldn't scream. I couldn't cry. I couldn't move. I couldn't do anything at all except lie in the ditch by the road and try to breathe.

I looked at the bull. He lowered his head and pawed the ground, daring me to cross back over to his side of the fence.

"I take it back," I gasped, looking the bull straight in the eyes. "You're not a wimp."

A few days after the Brahman bull, Jimmy and I walked over to the clubhouse. We still shook whenever we thought of our close call, but we were getting better. We could even laugh about it a little bit. Then we'd think about our third Challenge and all our laughs would disappear.

"So when are we gonna do step three?" Jimmy asked.

"How about Friday night?" I said, relieved it was only Monday. "We could do it Friday night and then on Saturday we could bury the box. How's that?"

"Sounds good to me," Jimmy said.

We had five days to wait, and every day I got a little more scared. I figured that if being chased by a bull almost gave me heart failure, the odds weren't very good that I would survive the third test. Looking back on it, I think it would have been better to get it over with sooner. Because all week long I kept thinking about Friday night and wondering if a person could actually get scared to death.

"Maybe we shouldn't do it," I said on Wednesday.

"A deal's a deal," Jimmy reminded me.

"I know," I said. "I'm just scared, that's all."

"It won't be so bad," Jimmy said.

"Not for you, maybe," I said. "You're used to looking out your window and seeing coffins."

The reason Jimmy was used to coffins is because he lived next door to Heavenly Rest Mortuary. You know: A mortuary's a place where you take people when they die. The bodies are fixed up to look nice and happy like they're going to a party;

then they're put in a coffin. After that, you have a funeral.

"I may see them coming and going," said Jimmy, "but I've only been inside the place once."

"You're sure people actually go coffin shopping in there?"

"Positive. I went with my parents to shop for Uncle Waldo's coffin. Mom and Dad didn't want to take me, but I said that since we lived next door, I really wanted to go." Jimmy shrugged. "So they took me along."

"They have a whole room just for coffins?"

"Yep," said Jimmy.

Jimmy and I saw each other all the time during that last week he was in Austin. Our parents were real good about that. We took turns spending the night at each other's house. The days were still crackling hot and most people didn't like to be outside. But Jimmy and I didn't care. One morning we packed a lunch and went

64

fishing over at the pond. When Jimmy and I fished, we cut the barbs off the end of the hook. That way, if we caught something, we could pull the hook out without hurting the fish. We got a gigantic catfish that day, but we threw it back, just like we always did.

Another day we rented all the Star Trek movies and watched them from start to finish. Another day we went swimming.

On Wednesday we started to fill in our clubhouse.

"Are you sure you want to do this?" Jimmy asked as we carried our shovels over to the empty lot.

"I thought about starting another club with someone else," I said. "I even went to the clubhouse yesterday when you were at the dentist. I was all alone and the place felt sad and empty, sort of like the cage in the corner of my room after Billy died."

"Billy was a great guinea pig," Jimmy said. "Do you still miss him?"

"A lot," I said. "He was a good friend."

Jimmy shoveled some more dirt into the

hole and then asked, "What do you think Marvin's going to do when he sees we've filled in the clubhouse?"

"I don't know," I said. "I haven't really thought about it."

"Maybe we should have let him see inside it just once before it disappeared," said Jimmy.

"No way," I said.

I could tell Jimmy felt a little guilty about taking Marvin's money for an old beat-up comic. But I didn't feel a smidgin of guilt. When I was four or five years old, Marvin would say things like, "Hey, Zander, I'll trade you my great big nickel for your tiny little dime." And, like a stupid idiot, I'd do it. I probably lost at least ten dollars that way. Marvin cheated me out of lots of money when I was little. And he hasn't stopped trying yet.

Jimmy and I spent all afternoon filling in the clubhouse dugout with dirt. I had forgotten what hard work all that shoveling is. We hadn't finished by dinnertime, so we had to go back Thursday morning to finish the job.

It was almost noon when we finally hauled the roof boards away and packed down the last of the dirt. Then we clasped our hands in our secret handshake and repeated our secret password.

"Hi Lo Ini Mini Ki Ki, Um Chi Chi E Wa Wa," we said solemnly. Then we took a dollar from the money Marvin paid for the comic and walked over to Bennie's Luncheonette and shared a chocolate fudge sundae with peppermint ice cream and sprinkles. That was our favorite. I haven't eaten one since.

We waited till Friday to buy the lockbox at the T G & Y, the only dime store in town. There were only three boxes left.

"What do you think?" Jimmy asked. "Blue?"

"Red. That will show up more. If we wrap it in plastic, it should stay red till we dig it up again."

"Okay," Jimmy said.

We paid for the lockbox with our saved-up and comic-sale money and then walked real slow all the way home.

"What do you think should go in the box besides our pledge?" I asked.

"I don't know," said Jimmy. "But it should be something important, something that means a lot to you and me."

"We'll have to think about it," I said. "We'll have to think about it real hard."

N I N E

By Friday I was a nervous wreck.

"What's the matter?" my mom asked at breakfast.

"Nothing."

"What are you planning to do today?"

"Nothing."

"And tonight?"

"I'm going to spend the night at Jimmy's."

"Will you be eating dinner there?" Mom asked.

"I'll ask," I answered glumly.

Later that morning, Jimmy and I found Mrs. Snyder in her sewing room.

"How do you like these?" Mrs. Snyder said with a great big smile, holding up a pair of pajamas she was making for Jimmy. "They're to replace the barnyard animal ones that disappeared."

Jimmy squirmed next to me and I was afraid to look at him. I just stared at these horrible new pajamas, which had cowboys all over them.

"Aww, Ma," Jimmy said, rolling his eyes and shaking his head. "Cowboys are what you make for five-year-olds. Even astronauts would have been better than *that.*"

Mrs. Snyder shook her head. "It was just such a nice, soft fabric. And it was on sale. But you're right. I should have asked you," she said. "I keep forgetting you're not little anymore and I need to check with you before I buy anything that you're going to have to wear."

She sounded sort of sad. But I thought Mrs. Snyder was pretty cool for saying that, even though she was probably used to goofing up. Because, no matter how hard she tried, there was just a little something wrong with almost everything Mrs. Snyder made on the sewing machine. It was either the wrong color or the wrong shape. Or it was too big or too little. When it came to sewing, she just didn't have the knack for getting things right. On the other hand, I admired her for hanging in there. She was definitely an optimist. That's a person who always looks on the bright side of things.

"Maybe your cousin would like these," Mrs. Snyder said, kind of pretend cheerful. "Goodness knows, moving to California will be hard enough for you. You shouldn't have to wear pajamas you hate."

Suddenly I said, "I'll take them. I think they're neat."

Jimmy looked at me like my brain was one can short of a six-pack.

"Why, it would be my pleasure to give the pajamas to you, Zander," Mrs. Snyder said. "I'll be sure to finish them before we move." Her face lit up like I'd just handed her a diamond as big as a baseball.

"Thanks," I told her. And, strangely enough, I meant it.

"Mom?" Jimmy asked. "Can Zander eat dinner with us tonight?"

"Sure. We're having pizza. Is that okay?"

"Yes!" we both said at the same time.

Now I have to tell you: There's no way we'd have pizza at my house. Too much cholesterol and fat. Mom is really into health food. If we ever had pizza, it would be made with steamed vegetables and tofu. The only reason she lets us eat eggs is because she claims they're a "perfect" food.

The Snyders were pretty cool. Especially Mrs. Snyder. Jimmy didn't know how lucky he was. I was going to miss all of them. I was going to miss them *a lot.*

At dinner, Mr. Snyder looked at me funny.

I wonder if he suspects, I thought, all of a sudden feeling guilty for something I hadn't even done yet. I smiled at him real casual and innocent.

"I know it's going to be hard on you boys when we move, Zander," said Mr. Snyder. "I just want you to know that you're welcome to come visit us in California anytime you want."

"Our house is just half a block from the beach and there's lots of stuff for you to do," added Mrs. Snyder.

I tried not to squirm.

"It sounds like lots of fun," I said politely.

"It's Venice Beach," said Jimmy. "My cousin says the place is loaded with nuts. Really zoned-out types. You know: 'Cool, dude, let's go catch some rays' kind of people. I hope you can come stay with me. We could have a great time."

"Yeah. Maybe next summer," I said, imagining all the different kinds of no good Jimmy and me could get up to in a place like that. I wondered if my parents would ever let me go so far away all by myself.

Even though Mrs. Snyder had made pizza, I could only push down one piece.

My stomach felt like a trampoline. Every time I swallowed I thought the food would bounce right up again.

"Are you all right, Zander?" asked Mrs. Snyder.

"Sure," I said, hating to lie to her. But since it was for the sake of being polite, I guess it was okay.

"You're not eating much. I've never known you to have only one slice of pizza."

"I'm fine. It was really delicious, Mrs. Snyder. But that was a big piece you gave me the first time, and I'm filled up already."

"Well, save a little room for dessert," she said. "I made something special just for you and Jimmy."

Swell, I thought. I tried to smile as I pictured my puke all over the table.

"What's for dessert?" Jimmy asked, all excited. I didn't understand how he could think of eating dessert when the third Challenge was just a couple of hours away.

"Pineapple upside down cake."

Now if there's one thing I love, it's Mrs.

Snyder's pineapple upside down cake. The cake is loaded with brown sugar and butter and it's the best in the whole world. Mrs. Snyder knew I loved it.

"Oh, boy!" I said, trying to sound real enthusiastic. "My favorite!" Oh, swell! I thought, trying to make the trampoline stop bouncing before dessert.

"I hope you fellas will be quiet tonight," Mr. Snyder said just before he went to bed. It wasn't even nine o'clock. "Try to keep your noise down to a dull roar, okay? I've had a long day and I need a good night's sleep."

"We'll be quiet," I said.

"We'll be quiet," echoed Jimmy. "I promise."

Around nine-thirty, Mrs. Snyder came into Jimmy's room to tell us good-night. "Now, you boys need to get some rest," she cautioned. "So don't stay up too late."

"We won't," we promised.

After the house was quiet, we watched

TV in Jimmy's room for a while. But I was so nervous I couldn't sit still.

Finally I asked, "Are you sure there's no funeral tonight?"

"I'm positive!" said Jimmy. "I told you already. People don't have funerals at night."

"But what about the embalming room? Maybe they're fixing up a body for a funeral tomorrow. Maybe they're dressing someone up in party clothes or something."

Jimmy shook his head like he was talking to a total dork. "The place is closed. Look out the window and see for yourself."

I stared out the window at the dark, shadowy house next door and wondered where the embalming room was. "What do they put inside the bodies to make them last?" I asked.

"I dunno," Jimmy said. "Some kind of preservatives, I guess."

"The same kind they put in bread and ice cream?" I asked.

"How would I know?" Jimmy said. "I never asked for the recipe."

"So we're going to do it in the display room?" I asked.

"Right. That's where the sample caskets are. All we have to do is pick one out and climb in."

"But first we have to get out of the house," I reminded him.

"I told you," said Jimmy. "That's easy. We'll use the back stairs."

Jimmy's house was a duplex, sort of like a two-family apartment building. The Hardwicks lived downstairs and the Snyders lived upstairs. At the back of the house there was an outside stairway, sort of like a fire escape, that led from the Snyders' kitchen door down to the ground. That's how we planned to sneak out of the house.

As I waited till it was time for us to go downstairs, I lay in bed and looked at the lamp shining on the fire-engine curtains. Lucky for Jimmy, they were leaving these behind. All his other stuff, his toys and books and Legos and things, was packed in boxes for the movers to carry away. There's something sort of sad about seeing people's lives stuffed and sealed in boxes. It's like part of them has disappeared.

"Do you believe in ghosts?" I asked Jimmy.

"Not anymore," Jimmy said.

"I know some grown-ups who believe in ghosts," I said. "What if they *do* exist? Do you think they'd be floating around in the mortuary?"

"I don't know," Jimmy said. "I doubt it."

I didn't like the way he sounded. He didn't seem confident anymore. Even though he was used to living next door to a mortuary, Jimmy had never done anything like *this* before.

"Have you ever known anybody who slept in a casket?" I asked.

"Nobody besides vampires," Jimmy answered.

"I'm sorry you said that."

"Me, too."

We must have fallen asleep. Because the next thing I knew, I was dreaming about vampires shaking me. Then I realized it was just Jimmy trying to wake me up.

"Psst! Zander! Wake up!" he whispered.

"Huh?" For a second I didn't know where I was. Then I remembered. And as soon as I remembered, I got this sick feeling in my stomach like when the dentist tells me I have a cavity.

"It's almost midnight," Jimmy said. "We fell asleep. It's a good thing I woke up."

"Yeah," I mumbled.

"Come on," Jimmy said. "Get out of bed. If we don't do this, we won't be Official Best Buddies Forever."

"Okay," I said, as I sat up and rubbed my eyes. "Are you sure we're doing the right thing? Maybe we need to think about it again. Maybe we need to—"

"What do you mean?" asked Jimmy. "We made a deal."

Jimmy stood up and tugged at his dinosaur pajamas. They were too big in the waist and he had to keep pulling them up. Jimmy said that when he first got the pajamas, the *Tyrannosaurus rex* gave him bad dreams for months.

"Are you ready?"

"Sure," I whispered, standing up. I think if I had been given a choice right then between doing our third Challenge or having a cavity filled without novocain, I would have chosen the cavity. "Best Buddies Forever," I said.

We looked at each other real carefully. Then Jimmy put his hand out for our secret handshake. His hand was wet and clammy, too.

"Let's go," Jimmy said.

We grabbed our ten-year-guaranteed, lithium-battery flashlights and tiptoed out of his room and down the hall to the kitchen.

"Are you hungry?" Jimmy asked when we got to the kitchen.

"Are you kidding?" I asked. I was so close to puking all over Mrs. Snyder's spotless kitchen floor that I was afraid to swallow my spit.

We sneaked out the back door and

closed it quietly behind us. Then Jimmy started down the stairs ahead of me. Suddenly something creaked. It sounded like a door opening. Or maybe a coffin lid.

My eyes opened wide. "What's that?" I gasped, holding my breath.

"Skip that step," Jimmy whispered. "It squeaks."

I nodded and let the air seep slowly out of my lungs.

The night was warm and cozy and crickets filled the air with their singing. Did you know crickets make that noise by rubbing their wings together? Marvin told me that. At least he's good for something.

On the way down the stairs, I decided I must be crazier than I thought. I mean, I thought it was important for me and Jimmy to be Official Best Buddies Forever and all that. But maybe being stampeded by a Brahman bull was enough. I won't ever forget that, I thought. I'm sure I won't. I don't have to spend the night in a casket, too.

Staying in the shadow of the Snyders'

house, we ran across the backyard, then sneaked right up to the back door of Heavenly Rest. "What now?" I whispered.

"We crawl through the cat door, just like I said," Jimmy answered.

Before it was a funeral home, Heavenly Rest Mortuary was a regular house. And the back door in the regular house had a door cut at the bottom for either a small dog or a large cat, I don't know which. Anyway, when the funeral people took over the house and converted it into a mortuary, they never bothered to change the back door. I guess they figured that there weren't any kids or animals stupid enough to want to sneak into a mortuary in the middle of the night and check out the dead bodies.

"What if we don't fit?" I asked.

"I already checked it," said Jimmy. "I measured the door and I measured me. It might be a tight fit, but we'll make it."

"Swell," I said. Then I managed to add, "You first."

Jimmy hiked up his pajamas and kneeled

down. Then he sort of scrunched himself together. First he put his arms over his head and stuck them through the cat door. Then his head disappeared. Then his chest. Everything went all right till he got about halfway through the door and it got to be a really tight squeeze around his bottom. That's when his pajama bottoms just sort of folded right off him as he wiggled through the door. I started to laugh. There he was, his butt as bare as the day he was born, wiggling as fast as he could through a stupid cat door.

"Oops!" I heard him say on the other side of the door. "I'm naked!"

He stuck his head through the opening and spied his pajamas. Then his head disappeared and his arm reached through the hole and grabbed them. After the bottoms disappeared, Jimmy stuck his head out again.

"Come on!" he whispered.

The inside of the funeral parlor was lit real dim.

"The caskets are that way," Jimmy whispered, pointing to the end of the hall.

I nodded silently, switching from thoughts of dead bodies to coffins.

We tiptoed down the long hall to a door at the end of the corridor.

"Here it is," said Jimmy.

"Are you sure this is the right room?" I asked. "It could be the embalming room. It might be filled with dead bodies lined up waiting for preservatives."

"I'm sure this is the right room," Jimmy said. "So go ahead and open the door."

"Not on your life," I said.

"Okay." Jimmy swallowed. "Then I'll do it."

Jimmy reached out and turned the knob. Then he opened the door a crack and shined his flashlight inside.

"This is it," he whispered, as he swung the door wide. The whole room was filled with coffins. It was a sight creepy enough to fade my freckles. I counted seventeen caskets, all of them with their lids open. I was surprised to see that coffins came in all shapes and sizes. Great place for a vampire party, I thought, as I imagined all these long-toothed, pasty-faced people sitting around in caskets telling garlic jokes and talking about bloody necks. Dressed in black capes and top hats, they'd argue about whether boys' blood tastes better than girls' blood while they nibbled on nachos and chips and ate pineapple upside down cake.

That's when I started to get *really* nervous. To be perfectly honest, my knees shook so hard I had to lean against the wall so they wouldn't fold right up under me like the legs on a cheap card table.

"Come on inside," Jimmy said.

"What if I need to pee in the middle of the night?" I asked. Actually, I needed to go right then. But since I had just done it before we came downstairs, I figured it would be pretty wimpy to admit I had to do it again so soon.

"We'll find the bathroom later," Jimmy whispered. "Let's take a look around now and choose a casket."

We stood right next to each other when we walked inside the display room. There were caskets everywhere, and the first thing I did was check to see if any of them were occupied. I shined my flashlight in one, expecting to catch sight of a vampire snoozing inside. Luckily, the casket was empty. The inside was covered with poofy satin, all soft and padded. It even had a pillow.

Do dead people feel? I wondered. Do they care whether their casket is comfortable? I guess so, I figured, or they wouldn't be padded. Or maybe nobody knows for sure. Maybe the casket's padded just in case.

Some of the coffins were fancy on the outside and some were plain. I was looking at one without much decoration when I noticed the price tag on it.

"Wow!" I said. "Three thousand dollars for a casket? It's just a wooden box with a little bit of decoration! It sure is expensive to die. Maybe I'll go into the casket-making business when I grow up."

"You could probably make a lot of money."

"At these prices, I'd be a millionaire."

"Maybe they have sales sometimes," Jimmy suggested.

"You mean like a Labor Day special on caskets? I don't know," I said. "I sorta doubt it."

"I suppose you're right. I guess it wouldn't be fair if some people died at sale time and others had to pay full price."

"One thing's for sure," I said. "If I went into the casket-making business, I'd never run out of customers."

"And they'd never run out on you, either," Jimmy joked. Then he got down to the nitty-gritty. "Which one do you want to sleep in?"

"I don't know. You choose first."

After we talked a little, we decided to sleep in caskets that were next to each other. That way, if we needed help, we could get it fast. Also, we decided to keep our flashlights on all night.

"What if they run down?" Jimmy asked.

His voice shook a little and I could tell he was scared, too. For some reason, that made me feel better.

"They're guaranteed," I said.

"But what if the guarantee's wrong?" he said. "What if our flashlights go out and we're stuck in the dark in a room full of caskets?"

"We'll write away and get our money back."

"No, *really*," he said.

"I don't want to think about it," I said.

"Me neither."

"Did you remember to bring the alarm clock?" I asked.

"Yeah."

"Then let's get started."

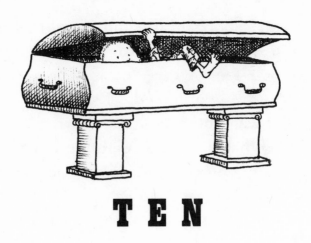

TEN

Jimmy and I had all sorts of trouble choosing which coffins to sleep in. We wanted to be next to each other. And we also wanted to be in the really expensive coffins, because they have more padding. So there we were, running around from coffin to coffin, shining our flashlights in every direction, poking pillows, grabbing tags and comparing prices just like our moms at a swap meet. It took us at least an hour to decide where we were going to sleep. When we finally settled on our choices, I slept in a $5,899 coffin and Jimmy slept in a $5,765 one. It was nice of Jimmy to let me sleep in the most expensive coffin. That's the kind of friend he is.

Then the real trouble began. Since the coffins were resting on stands almost as tall as my dining-room table, we had to climb up high to get in them. I could help Jimmy up, but then I was stuck, because I couldn't get into my coffin by myself. There was one chair in the room, over against the wall. Actually, it was a double chair, like a little sofa. It was big and heavy and we could barely move it. But we finally managed to push and shove the chair over next to my coffin. First I gave Jimmy a boost into his coffin. It was so wobbly we almost tipped it over. Then, after Jimmy set the alarm for five o'clock, I stepped up on the chair so I could climb into my own coffin.

Imagine: People actually spend almost six thousand dollars for a coffin. That's insane. All you do is stick it in the ground where it gets wet and dirty and rots away, so I don't know what difference it makes. Me, I'd just as soon have the cheapest one. Then my parents would have some money left over to take a long trip so they could get over grieving about me. It would probably take them a long time. I doubt if Marvin would grieve for me, though. Maybe he would. He'd probably miss having someone to tease and make miserable.

Even though I was really tired, I was so nervous it's a miracle I slept at all. I can't remember what woke me up. Probably just fear.

You know how it is when you wake up in the middle of the night and your room is all dark and even though you don't believe in monsters anymore, you just *know* there's a monster crouched under the bed or hiding in the closet waiting to grab you? That's how I felt when I woke up in the coffin—except a million times worse. I thought I had left my flashlight on, but it was pitch dark in there. I pushed the switch up and down, but nothing happened. Without any warning, a herd of butterflies sprouted in my stomach and flew around in every direction. Then the insects developed hooves and started to stampede. I'm actually gonna die from fright! I thought.

I guess it's convenient that I'm already in a coffin. I shook the flashlight a couple of times and suddenly it lit up. In my whole life, I can't ever remember being more relieved.

Unfortunately, light or no light, I was still scared. The room was totally quiet. I listened for ghosts and vampires as I shined the flashlight at the ceiling. I wished I had a blanket to cover me. When I'm sleeping in my room at home and I think there's a monster lurking under the bed, I always pull the covers up to protect me. But stuck in a coffin like I was, I didn't have anything to put between me and whatever was out there. I wondered why I hadn't thought of that ahead of time. I could have brought a blanket. But all I had was my flashlight, and that sure didn't feel like enough protection to me.

For one second, I thought about closing the coffin lid over me. But that was too creepy. So I lay on my back in the coffin and looked up at the faraway ceiling. It took hours for me to get the nerve to prop myself up on my elbow. I didn't have the slightest idea what time it was. I looked for a sliver of light sneaking through a crack in the curtains, but I didn't see one. I wondered if light would ever shine on me again.

I felt like my coffin was a tiny island in a forever ocean of dark. I don't think I'd ever really felt honest-and-truly alone until then. To tell you the truth, I hope I never feel like that again.

"Aiieeeee!" A muffled moan slithered soft and low out of the dark.

I froze.

Vampires, I thought. Pointy-toothed, pasty-faced, blood-sucking vampires.

"Ahhhhhh!"

I couldn't move, couldn't swallow. My lips were caked and as dry as a corn husk.

"Mmmmmmmm . . ."

It's a ghost, I thought. That must be how ghosts sound, all sad and lonely because they don't like being dead.

Quick, I turned off my flashlight and lowered myself into the coffin again.

"Ahhhhhh!" My fear worked itself into

a nasty ball right in the middle of my stomach. And then the ball slid up past my chest and into my throat, and I knew when it got to the top, it would change into a terrible, loud scream.

I opened my mouth.

Ding! Ding! Ding! Ding!

For a second, I didn't know what it was. Then I remembered the alarm clock.

"Pssttt! Jimmy! Turn it off!"

"Huh?" When I heard his groggy voice, I realized the moans and groans were his. He must have been having a bad dream.

Ding! Ding! Ding! Ding! Ding!

"Turn it off before somebody hears it!"

I listened as Jimmy moved in his coffin. Then the alarm stopped ringing.

"Jimmy!" I whispered. I propped myself up on my elbow again. "Let's get out of here!"

But Jimmy didn't answer. The only thing I heard was terrible, sickening silence.

They got him! I thought. It wasn't Jimmy who turned off the alarm. It was vampires! Then it came to me: Jimmy's deaf in his right ear. And I realized that, hidden down inside the coffin like he was, he probably couldn't hear me.

"Jimmy!" I whispered louder. "I gotta get out of this place right now!"

Jimmy's flashlight came on, lighting up the inside of his coffin with a spooky glow. Then it flickered on and off a couple of times as he sent me a message.

___ _._

"Wait just a minute!" I said. "I'll come help you get out."

The stand my coffin rested on was wobbly, and I didn't want to knock anything over. So I had to be real careful. I left the flashlight inside the coffin, then held on to the side as I eased my legs over the rim and put my knees on the top of the chair.

Creeeek! Thwonng!

Suddenly the stand began to vibrate and my coffin started to shake. Kneeling on the chair, I grabbed the coffin and held on tight till it stopped vibrating. As quickly as I could, I leaned over and grabbed my flashlight. Then I slid to the seat of the chair, stepped onto the floor, and tiptoed over to help Jimmy.

"Come on down," I whispered.

Jimmy's face popped up over the side of the glowing coffin. He looked like a ghoul rising out of a grave.

"It's not going to be so easy," Jimmy said, looking down at the floor. "This thing's not very steady."

"Just go slow and you'll be fine," I said.

Jimmy got on his hands and knees in the coffin, then hung one leg over the edge. It was a lot easier to get in than out. I tried to think of ways to help him. The chair was too heavy for me to move it alone, so I put my flashlight on the floor and cupped my hands together and formed a step for Jimmy's foot. Once his foot was in my hands, he put his other leg over the side. At that point, he was half in and half out, sort of standing with one foot in my hands while he hung over the side of the coffin.

"Here," he said, extending one arm behind him. "Take the alarm clock."

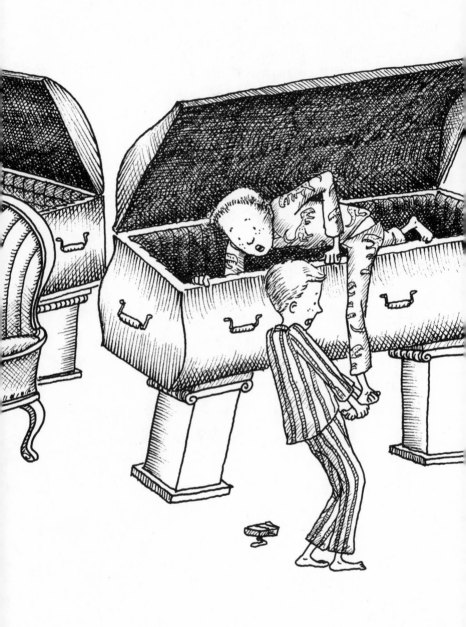

"I can't!" I whispered. "I'm holding you up." My hands began to wobble.

"I forgot."

Jimmy tried to hold the alarm clock and the flashlight in one hand and grab the side of the coffin with the other while he got all the way out so I could lower him to the floor.

Then my arms got tired and started to shake. I'm not really sure what happened next. I just know that Jimmy lost his balance and dropped the alarm clock and flashlight. When he grabbed the side of the coffin so he wouldn't fall, we both sort of collapsed and Jimmy fell to the floor with a thud!

Somehow, when he came down, he had given the coffin a tug. The wobbly stand started to sway back and forth, and the coffin on top was about to slide off and crash to the floor.

Quick as I could, I grabbed the side of the swaying coffin and hung on.

I couldn't see a thing. If the coffin crashed to the floor, the Snyders and Hardwicks would probably hear it all the way next door and they'd come running and find us, and we would owe the Heavenly Rest people almost $6,000 for a broken coffin. Then I'd have to work for the rest of my life to pay them back. And it would be hard to earn the money, because my parents would be so mad at me for sleeping in a coffin without permission that I wouldn't be allowed out of the house for a year.

"I think I'm bleeding!" Jimmy said from the floor.

I held on tight to the coffin as it swung back and forth.

"Forget the blood!" I hissed. "Stand up and help me keep this thing from slipping over the side!"

"But I'm hurt!" Jimmy said.

"I don't care if you cut your foot off! Pick it up and give me some help!" I whispered desperately. By then, I was clinging to that coffin for dear life. Every time it rocked, things got worse. Now, you probably don't know this, but coffins are extremely heavy. So every time the coffin rocked, it pulled me with it. I just wasn't heavy enough to keep it from sliding over the far edge and crashing to the floor. I needed Jimmy's help and I needed it right then!

"We're Official Best Buddies Forever now!" I croaked. "That means you gotta help me *now!*"

Jimmy shined his flashlight up at me.

What he saw got his attention real fast. "Oh, no!" he groaned, and shot up from the floor like a rocket. He got his hands on the coffin just in time.

"Hold on!" I said. "Hold on tight!"

The coffin was half on and half off the stand. Every time it rocked, the situation got worse. If we let go, it would crash to the floor for sure.

"Don't let go!" I hissed. "I'm going around to the other side."

"Okay," Jimmy groaned.

I ran around to the opposite side of the coffin.

"You pull and I'll push," I said.

We pulled and pushed and shoved and

wiggled with all our might. Suddenly the stand jerked real hard and began to vibrate.

"Yikes!" Jimmy said.

"Brace the stand with your foot!" I told Jimmy. "I'll do the same thing. Maybe that'll keep it steady enough to get this stupid thing back where it belongs."

We each shoved one foot against the cold, steel-tubed stand. Then we tried again.

"Ready?" I asked.

"Ready," said Jimmy.

Slowly, very slowly, we eased the coffin back to the center of the stand.

"Whew!" I said finally. "It looks okay to me. You all right?"

"I guess so."

"Get your flashlight and clock," I said. "Let's get out of here!"

We picked everything up, then ran out of the display room and took off down the hall like we were being chased by Darth Vader.

Jimmy was right beside me when I felt him lose his balance. I caught him just as he was about to crash into the wall.

I looked down. His pajama bottoms were hanging around his ankles.

"Take them off!" I whispered frantically.

He stepped out of his pajamas, picked them up, and ran down the hall half naked.

When we got to the cat door, I whispered, "You first!"

Holding onto his pajamas, Jimmy scrambled through the cat door, bare butt and all.

I followed as fast as I could.

Jimmy grinned at me as I stood up. He made an "okay" signal with his thumb and forefinger, then stepped back into his bottoms.

Staying in the shadows, we crossed into Jimmy's backyard, then crept back up the stairs to his house. We even remembered to skip the squeaky step. When we got to the top, Jimmy turned to open the door.

Whew! I thought. We did it!

"Oh, no," Jimmy groaned. "Oh, no!"

"What's wrong?" I asked.

His hand was on the doorknob. "I forgot to release the button on the knob. We're locked out!"

ELEVEN

After Jimmy and I realized we were locked out, we sat on the top of his steps and waited for his parents to wake up. It was one of those summer nights that are especially soft, so we weren't cold or anything. We were just scared.

"What are we gonna do?" I asked. "What if your mom goes in our room and finds us gone? She'll call my parents and then they'll call the police and then we'll be in one heck of a mess. They might even stop us from seeing each other again."

"I don't know what to do," said Jimmy. His voice sounded wobbly and strange.

"Don't you hide a key outside or anything?" I asked.

"I don't think so."

"What about a window?"

"Look around," said Jimmy. "The only windows into my house are a hundred feet off the ground. We'd kill ourselves if we fell."

"Yeah. You're right. You know how to pick a lock?"

"Nope."

"Me neither," I said.

"I guess we're done for," said Jimmy.

"Maybe so. Maybe not," I said philosophically.

I sat quietly on the step and thought about the fact that this was the next to last night I was going to spend with Jimmy. Just thinking about him leaving made me want to roll around in a puddle of sadness. I was really going to miss my friend. I couldn't imagine how I'd get to sleep at night without the signal from Jimmy's flashlight. After all, Jimmy in my life was a habit.

I had never watched a whole sunrise

from beginning to end. But since I was locked out of the house at five-thirty in the morning, and I couldn't go anywhere in my pajamas anyhow, it seemed like a good time to do it. Actually, I'm glad I did.

There was a smudge of purple and pink left in the sky, and a gold slice of moon still hung low over Lonnigan's barn, when Mrs. Snyder opened the kitchen door.

"What are you boys doing out here?" she asked in a real surprised voice.

"We got up early and came outside for a while," I said. Jimmy looked at me like he was waiting for me to tell a big lie. "The sun was rising and it was so pretty out here that we just sat down and watched the sky change colors."

"How nice!" said Mrs. Snyder. "Looks like it's going to be another scorcher today. Why don't you boys come inside and have some breakfast. How about blueberry pancakes?"

"Terrific!" said Jimmy with a wide grin. He poked me in the ribs with his elbow.

"Sounds great!" I said.

* * *

"We did it!" I whispered to Jimmy as his mom cooked pancakes.

"Yeah!"

I have to admit, I was pretty proud of myself. I had been feasted on by killer mosquitos. I had been chased by a Brahman bull. And even though I've never been more scared in my whole, entire life, I had actually spent the night in a coffin.

"Best Buddies," Jimmy whispered.

"Official Best Buddies *Forever*," I said.

We were still smiling when Mr. Snyder walked through the kitchen and kissed Mrs. Snyder on the cheek.

"Good morning, honey. Pancakes?" he asked. Then he glanced out the window.

"Umm." Mrs. Snyder smiled.

"I'll be back in a couple of minutes," Mr. Snyder said.

Jimmy and I kept sneaking peeks at each other as we set the table and then settled down to wait for breakfast. Just thinking about digging into a huge stack of pancakes made my mouth water. I figured maybe I could eat at least five.

Just as we had started to eat our pancakes, Mr. Snyder came back upstairs. He had a weird look on his face, like he had just seen a Martian.

"The strangest thing . . ." he said, shaking his head. "I saw the sheriff's car next door and went down to see what the trouble was. It seems someone broke into the mortuary last night and moved some furniture around and slept in some coffins."

"How could they tell that someone slept in the coffins?" asked Mrs. Snyder.

"Sheriff Kirkeby said the coffin pillows were mashed."

"Maybe it was vampires." Mrs. Snyder laughed.

I had to clamp my teeth closed real tight to keep my heart from shooting right out of my mouth. I couldn't look at Jimmy. I couldn't move.

"What do you suppose happened?" asked Mrs. Snyder.

"Nobody knows. The sheriff can't even figure out how the people got inside. All the doors and windows are locked. There's no sign of forced entry."

I glanced at Jimmy. Even though his face was almost buried in his pancakes, I could see he had turned bright red. Without ever looking up, he shoveled one dripping bite of pancake after another into his mouth with these real jerky movements, sort of like he was a mechanical doll.

Trying to be cool, I reached over and picked up my glass of milk. But my hand shook so bad I set the glass right back down. I noticed that Mrs. Snyder was watching me. Then she glanced at Jimmy. He was totally wacko. He looked like an eating robot.

She knows! I thought. I can feel it. She's got that look on her face. In just a second she's gonna tell Mr. Snyder that we were locked out. And then they'll put the facts together and figure everything out and then Mr. Snyder will lean out the window and call Sheriff Kirkeby and Jimmy and I will be arrested and taken to jail.

"The pancakes are great," I croaked.

"I made them just for you," Mrs. Snyder said with a big, suspicious grin on her face.

"You guys were so nice and quiet last night that I figured you deserved a treat."

"Thanks," I said, shooting Mrs. Snyder a grateful look. I was real glad I told her I'd like to have the cowboy pajamas she made. Real glad.

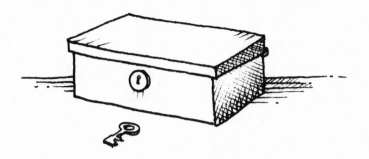

TWELVE

Jimmy and I sat all through breakfast pretending we didn't know anything. It was really weird. We'd be sitting there talking and all of a sudden Mr. Snyder would just shake his head and say, "I don't understand it. I just don't understand it."

"Me neither, honey," Mrs. Snyder would say sympathetically.

Jimmy and I didn't say a word. We finished our blueberry pancakes in silence. Then Jimmy gave me one of those looks that says "I gotta get out of here fast!"

After we thanked Mrs. Snyder for the

pancakes and were excused, we ran over to my house. As soon as we got in my room, Jimmy looked at me and started to laugh. At first it was just a giggle. Then I caught it. Soon we were laughing so hard we couldn't stop.

Then, wouldn't you know: Without any warning at all, nosy Marvin stuck his head through the door. "What's so funny?" he asked.

"Nothing," I said.

"Don't be stupid," Marvin said. "What's going on?"

"Nothing," Jimmy said.

"Well, I'll tell you one thing that's going on. You guys cheated me. The *Green Lantern* has a tear on the bottom of page fourteen."

"So?" I said.

"So?" echoed Jimmy.

"So I want my money back."

"No way!"

"You inspected it real carefully," Jimmy said. "You knew what you were buying."

"I didn't know it was in *that* bad a

shape," Marvin said. But I could tell he knew he couldn't win this argument.

"We didn't force you to buy it," I said, enjoying every minute of Marvin's mad.

Just then, I looked at Jimmy. I remembered the coffin and the sheriff again and started to sputter and laugh. As if it was contagious, Jimmy caught the laughing, too. That made Marvin *really* furious. I could tell by the look on his face, by his squinted eyes and pressed-thin lips, that he was madder than a wet hornet. I could also tell that deep down inside, he knew we had sold him the comic fair and square. Besides, I had a right to get even for the egg.

Marvin probably felt like a total idiot just standing in the doorway and watching Jimmy and me laugh. So he finally turned around and left the room, stomping down the hall like a crazed rhinoceros.

It took a long time for Jimmy and me to calm down. When we did, Jimmy asked, "You want to do the lockbox now?"

"I guess so," I said. "Except it's not a lockbox anymore. It's a time capsule."

"What are we going to put in it besides the pledge?"

"I don't know. What do you think?"

We didn't figure out what to put in the time capsule till after lunch. We thought about lots of different things, like our Boy Scout knives or our bug collection or our dried rattlesnake skin with the rattle still attached. But none of those were quite right. We finally settled on something perfect.

The next problem was where we were going to bury the time capsule. You have to be careful about choosing a place for something like that. Because if you choose the wrong spot, a stupid bulldozer's going to come along someday and dig it right up. Then everything is ruined.

See, the purpose of burying our time capsule was so Jimmy and I could come back eight years later and find it again. We had to make certain that the place we buried it wasn't scheduled to become a housing addition or a shopping center.

We thought a long time about the right spot.

"What about my backyard?" I said. "We're *never* going to move."

"That's what *I* thought," said Jimmy. "But what if you add on to the house or decide to build a swimming pool?"

"Bad idea," I said, nodding.

"How about down by the creek?" I said.

"Eight years from now, Cow Creek could be dried up. We have to find a place that's always going to be here no matter what."

"I've got it!" I said. "School!"

"Ugh!"

"No, it's not 'Ugh!' " I said. "Whether they want to or not, kids will always go to school. And, as long as Austin, Oklahoma, is here, some kids will be going to Grover Cleveland Elementary. And besides, I'll be going there for two more years and I can keep an eye on it."

"You're right!" said Jimmy. "Let's go."

*   *   *

115

In the back corner of the playground at Grover Cleveland Elementary is a huge old maple tree. Around the middle of October, people in town actually drive out of their way to see this tree. It's like a landmark. Nobody would ever let it get cut down. Every autumn, the leaves change to red and orange and gold. And when the leaves fall, the ground looks like a sunset slid to earth. That was the perfect place to bury our time capsule. It would be safe there forever, guarded by the most beautiful tree in the world.

After we picked up some shovels in my garage, Jimmy and I went over to the school yard. It was the end of vacation. Summer school was over and the playground was empty. We found the place that was hidden by a hedge and climbed over the fence.

"We gotta make a deep hole," I said. "We can't take the chance of some kids digging around in the dirt and finding our time capsule."

"Right," Jimmy said.

116

We chose a spot seven steps from the trunk of the maple tree and right under our favorite climbing branch. Years later when we came back, we'd know exactly where to look.

It took us till almost dinnertime to get the hole deep enough. We took turns digging, because the earth was hard and there were lots of roots in the way.

"It's gotta be this deep," I said, pointing to the top of my knee. I stuck my leg in the hole, and sure enough, the hole was as deep as my knee.

"It's done," I said. "Are you ready?"

"I guess so."

I climbed out and stood next to Jimmy. We opened the box together and Jimmy picked up the piece of paper that we had rolled up inside and tied with a piece of blue ribbon I got from my mom's gift-wrapping box.

It was our pledge. We wrote it ourselves in ink.

Jimmy unrolled the paper and started to read.

First of all, we are now Official Best Buddies Forever. For the rest of our lives we are tied together by our memories of weird deeds done. No matter how far apart we are. No matter how many years pass. We will always be Official Best Buddies Forever. And we pledge not to let anybody else ever take that place for the rest of our lives.

We pledge that if one of us is ever in trouble and needs help, we will be there no matter what.

And we also pledge to come back to this spot eight years from Today on September 1st. We will dig up this time capsule and find out if the ten-year guarantees on our special lithium-battery flashlights are really true. We are enclosing the guarantee slips just in case. If the batteries don't work, we can write away and get our money back.

Signed,
James Maxwell Snyder
and

Alexander Lain Caulfield

Jimmy folded the pledge up real carefully and put it in the red lockbox. Then we took out our flashlights. We flashed our last coded message together:

—··· · ··· —　　—··· ··— —·· —·· ·· · ···
··—· ——— ·—· · ···— · ·—·

After we finished, we put the flashlights in the box. We turned Jimmy's light on and left my light off as a test to see which one would be working in eight years. We put our pledge and guarantees in the box with the flashlights and then closed the lid and locked it.

We each took a key and solemnly shook hands in our secret handshake. Then we said "Hi Lo Ini Mini Ki Ki, Um Chi Chi E Wa Wa" for the very last time. That's when I started to cry. I could already feel the empty hole in my life that Jimmy's leaving was going to make.

"Don't forget to put your key in a safe place," I said. "We can't lose them."

"I'm tying it around the neck of my teddy bear. Even though I'm too old for stuffed animals, I'll always keep my teddy bear." Jimmy snuffled as he wiped his eyes. "I've had it since I was born." His tears washed streaks down his dusty, dirty face, painting sad stripes on his cheeks like a crazy zebra.

Now, I would never say anything to Jimmy, but I happen to know that every once in a while when he feels sad or lonely, Jimmy still sleeps with his teddy bear. I understand that. Sometimes old toys feel the best. It's like old friends.

It took me till Christmas to figure out where to put my key for good. That's because I didn't want Marvin to find it. He's a terrible snoop.

For a while I kept the key under my pillow. And then I hid it in one of my science fiction books. But now I'm making a special wooden box just to hold the key. The wood I'm using is maple. It will turn a real pretty golden color when I oil it. And I've discovered the perfect hiding place for the box. Marvin couldn't find it in a million years.

NOTE: Occasionally in this book there are some messages written in Morse code. Here's the code so you can translate the messages.

A	.—		N	—.
B	—...		O	———
C	—.—.		P	.——.
D	—..		Q	——.—
E	.		R	.—.
F	..—.		S	...
G	——.		T	—
H	....		U	..—
I	..		V	...—
J	.———		W	.——
K	—.—		X	—..—
L	.—..		Y	—.——
M	——		Z	——..